Parents and Caregivers,

Stone Arch Readers are designed to provide enjoyable reading experiences, as well as opportunities to develop vocabulary, literacy skills, and comprehension. Here are a few ways to support your beginning reader:

- Talk with your child about the ideas addressed in the story.

- Discuss each illustration, mentioning the characters, where they are, and what they are doing.

- Read with expression, pointing to each word. You may want to read the whole story through and then revisit parts of the story to ensure that the meanings of words or phrases are understood.

- Talk about why the character did what he or she did and what your child would do in that situation.

- Help your child connect with characters and events in the story.

Remember, reading with your child should be fun, not forced. Each moment spent reading with your child is a priceless investment in his or her literacy life.

Gail Saunders-Smith, Ph.D.

STONE ARCH **READERS**

are published by Stone Arch Books, a Capstone Imprint
151 Good Counsel Drive, P.O. Box 669
Mankato, Minnesota 56002
www.capstonepub.com

Library of Congress Cataloging-in-Publication data
is available on the Library of Congress website.
ISBN: 978-1-4342-2514-6 (library binding)
ISBN: 978-1-4342-3054-6 (paperback)

Summary: Jake wants to buy a gift for his teacher, Mr. Carter,
but he doesn't have any money. He calls the Pet Club into action,
and they have a pet wash to earn some money.

Reading Consultants:
Gail Saunders-Smith, Ph.D.
Melinda Melton Crow, M.Ed.
Laurie K. Holland, Media Specialist

Art Director: Kay Fraser
Designer: Emily Harris
Production Specialist: Michelle Biedscheid

Printed in the United States of America in Stevens Point, Wisconsin.
092010
005934WZS11

The Pet Wash

A **PET CLUB** STORY

by Gwendolyn Hooks

illustrated by Mike Byrne

STONE ARCH BOOKS
a capstone imprint

Meet the PET CLUB!

Lucy

Jake

Buddy

Ajax

Lucy, Jake, Kayla, and Andy are best friends. Lucy has a rat named Ajax. Jake has a dog named Buddy.

Kayla has a cat named Daisy.
Andy has a fish named Nibbles.
Together, they are the Pet Club!

Jake checks his calendar. The
big day is coming up.

Jake calls his friends. They can all come over.

"It's almost Mr. Carter's birthday,"
Jake says.

"We should get him a present,"
Andy says.

"He is our favorite teacher,"
Lucy says.

"And he helps us with the Pet Club," Jake says.

"But we don't have any money,"
Kayla says.

"Let's have a pet wash," Jake says.

"I'll bring a bucket," Andy says.

"I'll bring soap, combs, and brushes," Kayla says.

"I'll bring my special pet care kit," Lucy says.

The next day, Jake puts a sign in his yard.

Andy fills the bucket with water.
Kayla adds soap.

"I think we should start by
cleaning our pets," Lucy says.

"That's a great idea," Jake says.
"You're first, Buddy."

After Buddy is clean, Lucy is ready for him.

She is going to use her special
pet care kit.

"Lucy, are you finished yet?"
Jake asks.

"Okay," Lucy says. "Here comes
Buddy!"

"Buddy!" Jake shouts. "What
has Lucy done to you?"

"Don't worry," Lucy says. "Now
Buddy can help us."

Soon Jake is too busy to think about Buddy. The pet wash line is super long!

Finally, the last pet is clean.

"Our pet wash worked," Kayla says.

"And now we can get Mr. Carter a present," Lucy says.

"We sure can," Jake says. "But I'd like my old Buddy back first."

"I think the old Buddy is already back," Lucy says.

"That's my boy!" Jake says.

STORY WORDS

calendar   present   favorite

money   special   finished

Total Word Count: 283

Join the Pet Club today!

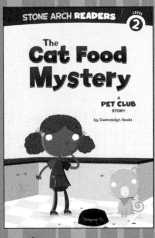

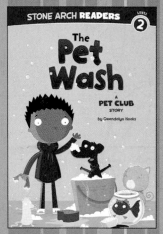